ASTEROID STRIKE

BY
MICHAEL
JOHNSTONE

ILLUSTRATIONS
BY ANDY DIXON

W
FRANKLIN WATTS
NEW YORK • LONDON • SYDNEY

When the world stood on the brink of the twentieth century, life had changed very little for most men and women during the previous hundred years.

True, more people were living in towns and cities and working in factories than there had been at the start of the nineteenth century. But the Age of Machines was only just starting.

Cars were for the very rich.

The first flight in a powered aircraft was still three years away.

Most people could only dream of owning a telephone.

Man on the Moon? Forget it!

The age of computers was almost a century down the line.

Today we use cars for even the shortest journeys and technology has been developed that allows us to tell them where we want them to go – and how fast.

We think nothing of boarding an aircraft and jetting off to the other side of the world.

Between 1969 and 1972 there were not one but twelve men on the Moon.

And we depend on computers for almost everything we do – in the office and in the home. We use them to access information on the Internet and to e-mail messages at the press of a key to friends thousands of miles away.

If we could have told all this to our great-grandparents when they were youngsters a hundred years ago, they'd have scoffed at us.

But these changes did happen. So imagine what our great-grandchildren will have to tell us if technology advances at the same rate in the next hundred years as it has in the last.

So let's take a peek into the future and enjoy an adventure set during the second half of the twenty-first century.

ASTEROID STRIKE

CHAPTER 1

Captain Luc Dupont was tired and being tired had made him irritable.

'I don't want you to come to me with problems, Lieutenant Mudrey,' he snapped at the fair-haired young officer standing in the doorway. 'If we have problems, I want you to bring me answers.'

'Yes, sir!' There wasn't a trace of an accent in Charles Mudrey's perfect English, something he had in common with most of the crew, and something that often annoyed Dupont. Luc spoke excellent English but with an obvious French accent.

Why, he had asked his wife before setting off for the launch pad all those weeks ago, was English the language of the European Interplanetary Space Agency? Why not French? Or German? Or Dutch?

'No, not Dutch, *chéri*,' she had said. 'Such a difficult language.'

'Anyway, Lieutenant, now you're here you may as well tell me what the problem is.' As he spoke,

Dupont put his elbows on his desk and began to rub the sides of his head with his fingertips.

'Are you all right, sir?' There was concern in Mudrey's voice. Dupont was a stickler for rules and regulations but he was a kind man, a good commander and popular with his crew.

'Bit of a headache, that's all,' Dupont said, looking up and smiling. 'Thanks for asking. What's the problem?'

'The temperature control in the Freezer Unit – '

'The one the serum's in?'

'Yes, sir. It's acting up – '

'Acting up?' There were some phrases Luc Dupont couldn't get the hang of. 'If we have to speak English at least make it understandable to a Frenchman like me.'

'Not working properly, sir,' laughed Charles, seeing the twinkle in Dupont's eyes. 'And we can't work out what's wrong. You're an expert – '

Luc shook his head. 'A Jacques of all trades, to adapt an English expression, and one you would like to help you.'

'If you would, sir,' said Charles. 'I've examined it over and over again and I can't see what's wrong.'

'And what makes you think my tired old eyes will see what your sharp young ones fail to spot?'

Charles laughed again. 'Because your "tired old eyes" as you call them are less than ten years older than mine. And because the brain behind them is reckoned to be the best there is.'

'It's amazing what flattery will achieve,' Luc grinned. 'Give me ten minutes and I'll be there.'

* * * * *

'Gotcha!' There was a note of triumph in Dupont's voice which was more than matched by the expression lighting up his face a few moments later when he crawled out from under the refrigeration unit in which the vital serum was locked.

'What was it?' Mudrey asked.

'Tiny hairline crack in the evaporator.'

'I looked there and didn't see anything,' Charles grimaced.

'You have to know precisely where to look,' said Luc. 'If you don't, you'd never spot it, it's so small. No one would.'

'You did.'

'Jacques of all trades can be masters of some,' smiled Dupont. 'Come on. Let's go eat.'

* * * * *

The dining room on the EISA Spacefreighter *New Millennium* was already packed when Dupont and Mudrey reached it. With a crew of over 250 and 1,500 paying passengers – mostly men, women and children emigrating to Mars to start a new life – there was hardly a vacant berth aboard.

'Who's at my table tonight, Joachim?' Dupont asked the chief steward.

'Mr and Mrs Davis, an American couple, and their twin sons, Samuel and Joshua. He's a doctor and she's a research chemist,' said Joachim, looking at the table plan. 'Professor Shultz and his companion, Miss Russell. He's with the Agency. Head of Human Resources. Not sure what she does. A Mr and Mrs Jackson, both teachers. Two children. And Eileen Constable, the singer.'

'How old are the twins?'

'Twelve going on eighteen,' grinned Joachim.

Dupont studied Joachim's seating plan for a moment, remembering precisely where everyone was sitting.

'And at mine?' Charles raised his eyebrows.

'Just Miss Munro – '

'Thanks, Jo,' said Charles, slipping a generous tip into the steward's waiting hand. '– as usual!'

CHAPTER 2

'Good evening! Good evening!' Luc smiled at the eager faces beaming at him.

'Good evening, Captain,' seven voices chorused back in unison.

'Hi!' said Sam Davis.

'Hello,' said his brother, Josh.

Luc sat down and smiled at the two boys. 'I know one of you is Sam and the other's Josh. But how do I tell which is which?'

'I'm Josh,' said one of the boys facing him across the round table.

'How *do* you tell them apart, Mrs Davis?' Luc turned to the woman on his right.

'Sam's got a slight gap between his front teeth – '

'And I've got a birthmark on my bum,' said the boy who had last spoken.

'Josh!' The man on the boy's right reprimanded his son. 'I'm sorry, Captain.'

Luc smiled. 'It's all right, Mr Davis. I've got two of my own – '

'What! Birthmarks on your bum?' said Sam, looking the picture of innocence.

'Sons!' laughed Luc. 'About your age.'

'So you're married?' the dark-haired young woman on Luc's left asked.

'*Bien sûr*, Madame Constable, of course!'

'Is she on board?' asked Profesor Schultz, a dumpy little man with cropped grey hair. He was sitting between Anne Davis and a slightly younger woman who Luc remembered was Manda Jackson.

'My wife? No,' said Luc. 'She hates space travel. We spent our honeymoon on the Moon, appropriately enough. However, she was sick throughout the entire journey.'

'I used to get space sickness,' said Manda Jackson, 'didn't I, dear?'

The man on Eileen Constable's left nodded.

'How did you get rid of it?' asked the heavily made-up blonde on his other side. 'I puke – sorry, get acute nausea. First thing every morning.'

Luc saw Professor Schultz glare at the woman and discreetly tap his upper lip.

'Silly me,' said Trixie Russell. 'I'm always doing that, aren't I, Schultzy? Forgetting to take my gum out.' Trixie took a blob of pink from her mouth and dropped it into the small black bag by her side plate.

'Went to a hypnotist,' Manda Jackson answered Trixie's question, trying not to laugh.

'Hypnotist!' said Eileen and Anne in unison. 'What happened? What was it like?'

Luc relaxed as the conversation got rolling.

'Tell me, Captain,' said Trixie after everyone had been served their first courses. 'There's no gravity in space, right?'

Luc nodded.

'So why isn't this soup floating out of the bowl?'

'We create artificial gravity,' Luc replied, wiping his mouth with his napkin. 'The ship is spinning round and round a central hub as we shoot through space. The further you are from the hub, the greater the gravity – '

'Could you run that past me again?' breathed Trixie, reaching into her bag and pulling out a lipstick.

'Centrifugal force,' Sam Davis broke in. 'If something is spinning very very quickly, it creates a force that pushes you away from its centre. We're so far from the central hub of this ship that we're being pushed to the floor. Right, Captain?'

'So how come I'm not dizzy?' asked Trixie. 'With all this spinning?'

'Not dizzy?' Sam muttered to Josh. 'I've never met anyone as dizzy as her before.'

'The Earth spins all the time and that doesn't make you feel dizzy,' said Anne Davis.

'Speak for yourself, honey!' Trixie giggled. She then turned to Luc and went on, 'Ndstru isthngsprd byncengy?' smudging her lips on her napkin as she spoke.

'Sorry?'

'Miss Russell was asking if it's true that the *New Millennium* is powered by nuclear energy,' murmured Professor Schultz.

'Shultzy!' Trixie dropped the napkin in her lap. 'I can speak for myself.'

'Partly,' said Luc.

'No, all the time!' pouted Trixie.

'I meant partly powered by nuclear energy.' Luc was only just winning his fight with a fit of the giggles, something Josh and Sam were obviously failing to do.

'Perhaps the children would like to be excused,' said Professor Schultz, glowering at them.

Children! I'll show him, thought Sam.

Luc carried on, 'When the booster rockets, the ones that give us lift-off thrust, separated from *NM* after we left the Moon, we used solar panels to generate power until we were deep enough in space for it to be safe to switch to nuclear power. Then we revert to solar energy when we're at cruising speed.'

'Nuclear power,' said Eileen. 'Isn't that dangerous?'

Professor Schultz shook his head. 'Not if it's controlled properly and the hull is protected,' he said. 'It has cut the journey time from the fifteen months it took to get from the Moon to Mars in the early days of this century to around three, three-and-a-half months today. Am I right, Captain?'

The *Amerigo Vespucci*'s done it in ninety-five days,' Sam Davis said, glaring at Schultz. 'It holds the Blue Riband for the fastest journey time from the Moon to Mars. It took it from one of your company's ships, didn't it, Professor?'

'What's the Blue Riband?' asked Trixie. 'Is that like a ribbon?'

'Yes,' said Luc. 'But only an imaginary one. Back in the early days of the 20th century, the fastest passenger ship to cross the Atlantic Ocean won the title. Nowadays it's the fastest liner to Mars instead.'

'And the *Vespucci*'s got it now?' asked Rowan Davis.

'Yes,' replied Luc. 'But it won't hold the record for long.' His lips tightened. 'I'm aiming to do it in under ninety this trip.'

'Isn't that foolhardy, Captain?' There was a chill in Schultz's voice.

'Not at all, Professor,' said Luc. 'Not at all.'

'But surely, Captain,' Professor Schultz said softly, 'to do that you'll have to average, let me see – '

'Around 960,000 kilometres a day,' Sam interrupted.

'Precisely,' the Professor nodded. 'And that means travelling at – '

'40,000 kilometres an hour,' said Sam.

'Mach 33.' Schultz glared at the boy.

'Sorry, Professor,' Sam said. 'Because there's no atmosphere in space, Mach isn't used to measure speed after Mach 26.' He turned his head and looked at Trixie. 'If we'd launched from the Earth and not the Moon, we'd have stopped using Mach to measure speed when we left our atmosphere.'

'What's this Mach guy got to do with things?' Trixie asked.

The professor cleared his throat but Sam beat him to it. 'It's a measurement of speed relative to the speed of sound – '

' – which travels at roughly 1,200 kilometres an hour,' the professor ran the words together. 'Which –'

'– is the equivalent of Mach 1.'

Trixie looked at him, amazed.

'So Mach 2 is 2,400 kilometres an hour,' Sam said quickly, before the professor could open his mouth. 'Three 3,600, and so on.'

'Is that a fact?' said Trixie blankly as Schultz slumped back in his chair.

'Game, set and match to Samuel Davis,' muttered Sam's brother.

Victory his, Sam couldn't resist the temptation to show off. 'It was invented by an Austrian called Ernst Mach – '

'1838-1916,' Josh added without looking up from his plate.

'Isn't it about time you boys went to bed?' snapped the professor.

'Schultzy!' Trixie scolded him. 'These kids are fascinating me. I didn't know anything could travel faster than sound.'

'Light does,' said Josh, his eyes still firmly fixed on his plate.

'Gosh.' Trixie's eyes grew wide. 'That must mean you can see yourself talking before you can hear what you've said!'

Josh looked up and glanced around the table.

'Mom,' he said, 'why's Dad got his napkin stuffed in his mouth?'

'Excuse me, sir.' The chief steward tapped Luc on the shoulder.

The Captain looked around, shaking with laughter like everyone else at the table apart from Trixie and Shultz. 'Yes, Joachim?' he managed to say.

'There's a message from Central Navigation

Control, sir,' Joachim said. 'Would you contact them right away?'

'Nothing serious, I hope,' said Rowan Davis.

'I shouldn't think so.' Luc smiled reassuringly as he rose to his feet. 'Excuse me for a moment.'

Sam and Josh watched the Captain stride to a now-empty table at the far end of the dining room, take his mobile from his pocket and key in a code.

A few moments later he was back.

'I'm afraid you will have to excuse me for longer than I thought,' he said. 'Nothing to worry about.' The same reassuring smile. 'A slight glitch in one of the navigation system's back-up computers.'

Luc turned to the Chief Steward who was hovering behind him. 'Joachim,' he said, 'as I may not be back in time for coffee, please arrange for everyone around the table to dine with me again another night.' And grinning at Trixie he went on, 'I have so enjoyed the company.'

* * * * *

'Now then.' Luc's voice was stern. 'What's all this about?'

Luc had not been truthful when he'd said there was something wrong with one of the computers. They were all in perfect working order.

'What did the signal say?' Luc went on. 'Exactly?'

'It's over there.' Giovanna Lorenzia, *New Millennium*'s Senior Navigation Officer, pointed to a printout on her desk. 'Best if you read it for yourself.'

When he had finished, he looked up.

'It means we'll have to slow down,' she said.

'We can't!'

'Captain,' she said crisply. 'We have to. If we don't *New Millennium* could be blasted into kingdom come.'

'I said we can't.' Luc could feel every eye in the room staring at him as the words shot from his mouth. In the stunned silence that followed, the usually inaudible hum coming from the bank of computers could clearly be heard.

'Captain!' Giovanna's voice shattered the stillness. 'We daren't take the risk.'

Luc Dupont's steely blue eyes locked into hers. 'We have to,' he said quietly. 'We have no choice.'

'Captain.' The Senior Navigation Officer held the Captain's piercing stare. 'The signal you're holding is telling us that we're heading straight for an exceptionally wide asteroid rush.'

'I can read, Lieutenant.'

Unfazed by the tone of Luc's voice, Giovanna went on, 'If we don't slow down, everyone on board could be killed. These things can be enormous. Some are hundreds of kilometres across.'

'I am very well aware how big asteroids can be.' The chill in Dupont's voice would have frozen salt water.

'Sir,' Giovanna was not to be put off. 'Even if we collided with a small one – one about the size of a house – at the speed we're travelling . . .'

She left the end of the sentence hanging in the air but, even so, everyone listening was only too well aware what would happen. If *NM*'s fuselage was pierced, at best the ship would be crippled and months would be added to the journey time; at worst it would spell instant death for everyone on board.

'Captain,' Giovanna broke the silence her words had created, 'the danger area is, what, two-and-a-half, three million kilometres ahead. Maybe more. If we carry on at this speed we will cruise into it in around three days. To be absolutely safe we have to reduce our speed to half. Less, maybe.'

'Maybe we should stop completely,' suggested Second Officer David Gillespie, 'until the asteroids are clear of our flightpath.'

Giovanna Lorenzia smiled at him. 'That's going a bit far, Davie. But if we aim to reach the area in six or seven days, longer if possible, we'll be in absolutely no danger. The asteroids will be well clear of our flightpath,' she added, then turned to Dupont and went on, 'We have to slow down, sir. There is no alternative.'

'There is always an alternative.' Luc's words came out very slowly.

'What?' The word shot from her mouth. 'What on earth's the alternative?'

'To increase speed so that we leave the danger area before the asteroids are forecast to arrive there.'

'We're already cruising at 40,000 kilometres an hour – maximum recommended cruising speed, hoping to get the Blue Riband from *Amerigo Vespucci*!' Giovanna's eyes narrowed. 'To reach the danger zone and be clear of it before the first asteroids get there, and give ourselves a decent margin of safety, we'd need to cover 3,500,000 kilometres in, say, 65 hours. We would need to increase speed to fifty-three thousand – '

'Eight hundred and forty-six k's,' said Luc.

'34.6 per cent,' added Davie Gillespie, in a tone that suggested that Giovanna and Luc weren't the only ones with calculator-sharp brains.

'That would be madness,' said Giovanna.

Luc turned away from Giovanna and looked at Cor van Boven, *New Millennium*'s Chief Engineer.

'How about it, Cor?' he said. 'Could we up it?'

The Dutchman scratched his chin. 'Theoretically, yes,' he nodded. '*Theoretically* we could maintain that speed for that length of time by increasing the frequency and strength of the controlled explosions we set off to generate nuclear power. *Theoretically* the ship would take the strain.'

'There's a but in your voice.'

'Yes,' said Cor. 'Not one. Two!'

'Which are?'

'If we do it,' van Boven's voice was calm, 'we increase the risk of a radiation leak. That could give everyone on board a bad dose of radiation sickness.'

'That's curable nowadays,' said Luc. 'Has been for years. What's your second but?'

Cor looked away from the Captain's gaze. After pursing his lips, he said, 'At that speed, if the fission-control computer miscalculates by as little as a mere fraction of a megawatt, it won't be an asteroid that'll get us, it'll be one almighty nuclear flash.'

The Captain clasped his cupped hands in front of his mouth, and time seemed to stand still as he blew softly into them, thinking hard.

'Check the calculations,' he said eventually to Cor. 'Make sure our safety margins are adequate.'

And as Cor's hands flew across his computer keyboard, Luc turned to Giovanna and went on, 'Plot a new course to take account of a proposed 34.6 per cent increase in speed for 65 hours.'

'Captain,' Giovanna was struggling to control her temper. 'This is suicide. Are you so obsessed with beating *Amerigo Vespucci* and getting the Blue Riband that you will risk the lives of over seventeen hundred people?'

Luc clenched his fist, crumpling the piece of paper in his hand in frustration. 'I couldn't give a toss for the Blue Riband. Will you do as I say?'

'And if I don't?' The challenge to Luc's authority in Giovanna's voice was plain.

'I will have no choice but to put you on a charge.'

Cool French eyes stared into blazing Italian ones.

It was Giovanna who spoke first. 'I would like it entered in the log that I advised against the course of action you want us to take,' she said, in a voice that would have chilled a fresh chicken.

'That's your privilege, Lieutenant,' Luc said in a voice that would have chilled it even more. 'I shall do as you request. And now, will you do as *I* request and plot that course?'

'Yes, sir!'

'Thank you.'

The tall, slim woman strode across Central Navigation Control and sat holding her back ramrod stiff in the chair facing a bank of computer screens ranged down the left wall. Even from behind, her fury was obvious as she brought up information on a small screen to her right. Then, she inputted it on the touch-sensitive screen in front of her.

A green grid glowed on the large screen just above her eye level. At the bottom right, a tiny image of the Moon shone silver. Diagonally opposite, at the top of the screen, Mars burned bright red. Between the two planets a tiny silver dot representing *New Millennium* moved along the spidery orange trail that indicated the existing flightpath.

'Why are you on manual?' Luc wanted to know. 'What's wrong with voice-activated commands?'

Giovanna turned round and glared at the Frenchman. 'It's safer.' She spoke slowly as if she were talking to a troublesome child. 'Keying in co-ordinates by hand eliminates the risk of computer miscomprehension.'

'These computers . . . ' Luc began.

Giovanna didn't give Luc a chance to finish what he was going to say. 'These computers can sometimes be disoriented by different accents, no matter how slight.' Her lips curled slightly. 'You must know that.' The slight emphasis she put on the word 'you' made Luc's hackles rise. He clenched his fists, anxious that his snappy Senior Navigation Officer should not see how much she was getting on his nerves. 'And on something as sensitive as this . . . ' Her voice trailed off as a sudden movement on screen caught everyone else's attention.

'Here come the asteroids,' said Giovanna, turning back to look at what was happening.

A golden trail cut across the *NM*'s path about halfway between its present position and Mars. 'If we maintain present speed – '

Every eye in the room watched the Spacefreighter cut a swathe through the asteroids' path before exploding and vanishing from the screen in a cloud of silver stardust.

'– we will arrive at the outer edge, the danger zone, allowing for a small margin of error in the information we have, sixty-eight hours from now.' Giovanna's voice was quite steady.

As she spoke, she keyed in more numerals and co-ordinates. 'If we reduce speed – '

'I told you to account for a 34.6 per cent increase in speed.' Luc's voice shook with anger.

'This is insubordination.'

'Not at all, Captain.' Giovanna's voice didn't waver for an instant. 'I intend to do just that. I am simply exploring all sides of the equation as I was trained to do in emergencies. Surely you must be aware of that, sir. It is standard procedure after all.'

Luc had to bite his lip to stop himself exploding with anger.

'If we reduce speed by half – ' Giovanna went on.

On screen, the tail of the asteroid stream was well clear of New Millennium's flightpath long before the spaceship was anywhere near the danger zone.

'– we will be perfectly safe.'

Her fingers flashed across the line of glowing

boxes running along the top of the screen once more before she said, 'And if we increase speed as the Captain wishes – '

The silver dot shot towards its destination, clearing the danger zone well before the head of the asteroid rush crossed its tailstream.

'– we will be safe . . .'

'Thank you,' said Luc.

'. . . assuming the nuclear reactors don't blow,' spat Giovanna. 'Only a lunatic would take that risk.'

An intense silence followed her words.

'I just happen to think – ' Luc began, then stopped for a second before going on, 'I just happen to think that putting seventeen-hundred-odd lives at risk is worth the gamble when you consider the alternative available.'

'Which is?'

'The lives of the twenty thousand miners and settlers already on Mars.'

'What?'

'Lieutenant Lorenzia, we are not just carrying passengers, mining equipment and other cargo,' said Luc. 'Some time ago doctors on Mars reported that people there were coming down with a virus, which attacks the central nervous system, paralyses digestion from mouth to gut and makes it impossible for those afflicted to eat or drink anything for themselves.'

'So they have to be fed by drip?' someone said.

Luc nodded. 'But not for long. Death is more or less inevitable.'

Luc stopped and looked from face to face before going on, 'So far they've managed to contain it to just a few cases by putting those affected into quarantine.'

Every eye in the room was now on the Captain.

'Microbiologists on Earth have succeeded in isolating the virus,' he went on. 'It's related to rabies.'

'Isn't that spread through saliva?' Cor asked.

'Rabies is, yes,' Luc nodded. 'But this variant is airborne. It seems that a rabid animal – probably a rat – stowed away on board a spaceship. And somehow a mutant strain was created when it reached Mars.'

'I still don't see what the hurry is,' said Giovanna.

Luc sighed. 'The experts have developed a serum. We have the first batch on board. It won't save the people already infected, but it will immunize everyone else.

'Computer projections of the way this bug multiplies show that if we don't get the serum to Mars to get mass vaccination underway within hours of our scheduled arrival time, the virus will have spread out of control. And that could mean 20,000 deaths. That's why we can't slow down. Satisfied?'

Luc Dupont sounded calm when he gave the order to increase speed by 34.6 per cent for 65 hours.

Cor van Boven sounded confident when he transmitted the Captain's wishes to Reactor Control, where astonished crew members looked at one other in amazement.

Giovanna Lorenzia's hand was steady as she keyed in *NM*'s newly confirmed flight path.

But Luc's mind was a-buzz with what-ifs. *What if I've made a mistake? What if whoever projected the asteroid's course miscalculated? What if the fission reactors crack under the strain?*

And Cor van Boven's confident tone disguised a deep-seated fear that if anything went wrong it would be he who carried the can. After all, who had told the Captain that it was possible to increase *NM*'s speed? Cor van Boven, that was who.

Giovanna's hand was steady because she knew she had done everything by the book. She might have questioned a superior officer's order; she had every justification in doing so. And if things went wrong, she could rightly claim that she had given Luc Dupont all the information he had needed to make whichever decision he came to.

'Pre-lunch swim, Miss Russell?'

Sixty-two hours had passed since Luc had given the order for the *New Millennium* to flash through space at mind-bending speed.

Not that the passengers had noticed, for not even the slightest tremor had heralded the dramatic increase in thrust. Or if they had, they hadn't said anything.

Trixie Russell looked at her watch. 'Captain,' she said, 'it may be pre-lunch to guys like you and Schultzy. To me it's pre-breakfast. I take a dip this time every morning in your fabulous pool as soon as I get up. Never see you there, though.'

'The crew has its own pool,' smiled Luc. 'Not quite as splendid as the one you use, I'm afraid.' *NM*'s passengers' gravity-free pool was set in a constantly revolving drum that kept the water against the side. Older passengers loved the way they could dive into the warm water and dive out of it. Children whooped with glee as they took armfuls of water and threw them across to the other side.

'I'll walk with you if I may,' Luc said to Trixie Russell. 'I always enjoy watching what's happening in the pool. It's relaxing.'

'Hi, Captain!' The Davis twin approaching *NM*'s first officer and Trixie gave the captain a mock salute.

'Morning,' said Luc, returning it.

'When are we all going to have dinner with you again?' the boy asked, smiling at Trixie. 'We had a great time two nights ago.'

'Tomorrow, I believe,' said Luc. 'I'm looking forward to it.'

'What have you two been up to, Sammy?' Trixie asked, seeing the racket bag slung over his shoulder. 'Or is it you, Josh?' she went on, frowning. 'Smile again, won't you, so I can see if you've got a gap in your teeth. I didn't notice a second ago.'

'There is another way of telling,' the boy said, smiling and tugging at the belt round his waist.

'Don't you dare,' laughed Luc, shielding Trixie's eyes with his left hand.

'I've been playing low-gravity tennis with Josh,' said Sam, grinning widely to reveal the slight flaw in his otherwise perfect teeth. 'You should try it, Trix. It's ace. Which is more than can be said for Josh's serving.'

'Where is he?' asked Trixie. 'Josh?'

'He's gone to the trampoline room ... '

'I've been there,' said Trixie. 'It was like bouncing around inside a huge rubber ball ... '

'That's 'cos it *is* bouncing around inside a huge rubber ball,' laughed Sam. 'Anyway, I'd better go. I want to have a shower before lunch. See you.'

'See you, Sammy,' said Trixie, taking Luc's arm as

Sam darted down the passage. 'Gosh, Captain,' she sighed, 'don't you wish you were twelve again, and had your life ahead of you?'

Luc thought to himself for a moment then shook his head and was about to say no when there was a sudden shudder and the lights flickered for moment.

It was just after noon plus five.

'What was that?' Trixie said. 'It reminded me – '

Luc never heard what it reminded her of because she was cut short by a sharp whistle that seemed to come from somewhere under the cuff of his tunic.

'And what was that?' asked Trixie. 'You got a bird or something up your sleeve?'

'Just my pager, Trixie,' said Luc, drawing his sleeve up to reveal a watch-like device strapped to his wrist.

'Why's it flashing red?' Trixie drew away from the captain.

'Not important,' Luc smiled. 'My Number Two needs to talk to me, that's all.'

And nothing in his voice betrayed the fact that an alert of some sort was underway.

CHAPTER 7

Luc strode into Central Navigation Control to be met by a white-faced van Boven, a wide-eyed Davie Gillespie and an open-mouthed Giovanna Lorenzia.

'What is it?' Luc's voice was tense.

It was the Italian Senior Navigation Officer who answered. 'Whoever plotted the asteroids' path got it wrong,' she said quietly, without a trace of the triumph she usually found hard to conceal when pointing out someone else's mistakes.

'What do you mean, got it wrong?'

'Either that,' said Giovanna, 'or Chief Engineer van Boven's reactors gave us less thrust than he thought.'

'There's nothing wrong with my nuclear reactors.' There was an edge in the Dutchman's voice.

'Let's leave backbiting to the politicians,' said Luc wearily. 'I want to know what has happened.'

'We've been hit by an asteroid!' said Giovanna.

'What!' The word shot from Luc's mouth. 'We can't have been. Our calculations were pinpoint accurate. Even after I gave the order, I checked them over and over again. I . . .'

His voice trailed off as he gazed at the three faces staring back at him. His eyes settled on Davie Gillespie. 'What's the damage, Davie?' he asked.

'Nothing terminal,' he replied. His slow, deliberate Scottish way of speaking made him sound calmer than he felt. 'It must have been tiny. No bigger than a marble. However, one of the solar panels has been knocked out. Thank the Lord it didn't pierce the main fuselage. If it had – '

'Repairable?' Luc cut him short.

Davie shook his head. 'No,' he said. 'Knackered.'

Luc turned to his chief engineer. 'What'll that do to our speed?'

'Slow us a bit.' Cor van Boven shrugged his shoulders as he spoke. 'We'll still get the serum to Mars on time. We've got another seven solar panels – we can function on less than that. And the reactors won't have been affected at all.'

'Thank goodness for that.' Luc puffed out his cheeks. 'What are the chances of being hit by another asteroid?'

It was Giovanna who answered his question. 'We should be safe,' she said. 'The asteroid rush is within telescope range. Look!' She turned away from Luc and, speaking into the microphone attached to the computer in front of her, said, 'Bring up Third-Gen Hubble Junior transmission sequence nine eight zero zero – three. No, zero four. Sorry.'

'Apology accepted,' a metallic voice from within the computer sniffed. The screen flickered for a second before filling with a crystal-clear image of

what looked like stationary lumps of rock.

But Luc was only too well aware that these rocks weren't immobile, but hurtling through space at unimaginable speed.

'How long before they cross our tailstream?' he asked. 'At least I hope it's our tailstream and not our flightpath if we have to reduce speed.'

'We'll be all right, Captain,' said Giovanna without taking her eyes off the numbers flashing on screen. 'Your original calculation was 100 per cent accurate, by the way.'

'Then if I calculated correctly,' Luc sounded puzzled, 'if Cor's instruments were accurate and we were doing the right speed – and you plotted the course properly, Lieutenant,' he added quickly as Giovanna spun round and glared at him, 'if everything was OK then how come we were hit?'

'Looks like it was a rogue one,' said Davie Gillespie. 'Blazing its own trail, so to speak. Not part of the rush we were warned about. Let's just thank Him Upstairs it was only a wee tiddler.'

'I don't believe it.' Luc banged the fist of one hand into the palm of the other. 'I just don't believe it. What are the chances of being hit by a rogue asteroid? Millions to one,' he went on, answering his own question. 'It must be. Oh well, there was nothing anyone could have done. These things appear from nowhere. At least we won't be hit by another.'

* * * * *

It was Junior Ensign Paddy O'Dwire who should have spotted it. And he would have if he hadn't sneezed three times in quick succession.

For it's impossible to sneeze and keep your eyes open at the same time.

And unfortunately seconds after noon plus five, Paddy O'Dwire sneezed, sneezed and sneezed again at the precise moment one of the numbers on the bank of digital displays on the screen in front of him changed.

Normally, the keen young nuclear physicist would have spotted any alteration as soon as it happened and taken the appropriate action. However, by the time he was over his brief sneezing fit, the digital display had settled and was quite still. There was nothing to suggest it had changed. It was just one unflickering figure among a hundred others.

Unfortunately for everyone on board *New Millennium*, the display that had changed showed the angle of the directional thrust being generated by the fission reactors.

Had the alteration, which had been caused by the asteroid strike, been noticed within half an hour a correction could have been made.

At any time in the thirty minutes after impact the thrust director could have been returned to the right angle and the accidental change would have had only the smallest effect on things.

But no one noticed in time.

Nobody realized that *New Millennium* was heading for disaster.

CHAPTER 8

'Captain! Something peculiar's happening.' Giovanna Lorenzia sounded concerned.

'Be right there, Lieutenant,' said Luc, swivelling round in his chair. 'What is it?'

He walked across to the main navigation computer, where Giovanna was standing.

'What's the trouble?' he asked when he was by her side, looking at the computer screen.

'This,' said Giovanna, highlighting the silver dot that indicated *New Millennium*.

Captain Dupont watched as line after line of figures appeared at the bottom of the screen.

'Look!' she said, highlighting a section. 'If we're on the course I set – the one we should be on – our ETA should be 00.45 Northern Mars Time April 2.'

Luc grunted.

'But according to this data, at a quarter to one that morning we'll be 100,000 km above Mars, flying past it, not towards it!'

'That's not possible.'

'That's what I thought,' said Giovanna. 'I've checked it three times. I know I'm right.'

'Davie! Over here. Quick!' barked Luc. 'And you, Cor.'

Three pairs of anxious eyes watched Giovanna

bring on screen all the data that proved her correct.

'There can only be one explanation for that.' The blood drained from Davie's face. 'One of the thrust directors is out of alignment with the others and has been for longer than's good for us.'

Luc shot across the office to the master computer. No sooner had he keyed in his password than the computer asked him to say, 'Mary had a little lamb.'

'Mary had a little lamb,' said Luc impatiently.

'Repeat,' said the computer.

'Mary had a little lamb.' Luc spoke much more slowly this time, a clear pause between each word.

'Thank you, Captain,' intoned the computer. 'You may proceed.'

Luc told the computer precisely what he wanted. A few moments later, the screen was filled with what to an inexpert eye must have looked like a nonsensical jumble of graphics and numbers, but which made absolute sense to NM's captain.

'It's Number Three,' he called out a moment or two later. 'It's thrusting at 48 degrees!'

'What should it be?' Davie asked grimly.

'38 degrees!' Cor van Boven gulped. 'No wonder we're going off course.'

'Who's on duty down there?' Luc turned to Cor who touched the 'Duty Rota' box on a small screen by his left hand.

'Junior Ensign Patrick O'Dwire. 6751.'

'Paddy!' Luc was astonished. 'He was the top nuclear-physics graduate in his year.' As soon as the words had tumbled from his mouth, Luc tapped '6751' on one of the displays on his main screen.

'Sir!' The surprise in the young man's voice was clear as it came down the line.

'Number Three directional thruster's firing ten degrees off true.'

'Can't be, sir,' the Junior Ensign sounded relaxed. 'Nothing's changed since – ' The confidence evaporated, replaced by panicky spluttering. 'Oh my – How the – '

'Stop whimpering and correct it.'

'Right away, sir.' There was a slight pause, then, 'Done it!'

'Report to my office the moment you're off duty.'

'Sir!'

* * * * *

But the damage had been done. Even as Luc Dupont sat back in his chair, wiping a bead of sweat from his brow, a tiny hairline crack appeared on Solar Panel Number 2 and began to spread, widening fractionally with each millimetre it grew.

CHAPTER 9

The second solar panel shattered at 14.30. It had such force that, in the pool, a huge swell of water shot across the void in the middle, almost drowning the divers caught unaware in its flow.

In the dining room Professor Shultz impaled his upper lip on the fork in his hand.

In the crew's wardroom, crew members turned to one another, the same question on everyone's lips. 'What in the name of the rings of Saturn was that?'

In Central Navigation Control more or less the same question shot from Luc's mouth but in such crude French that Giovanna, who was fluent in the language, blushed.

'Sorry!' gulped Luc, as Davie Gillespie turned from the screen he had been working at and said, 'Captain. Solar Panel Two has blown!'

Just then someone buzzed for permission to enter CNC. Luc glanced at the screen above the door, saw Charles Mudrey waiting, and pressed the lock release.

'I thought you were off duty?' Luc's voice was crisp.

'I am, sir.' Charles nodded. 'I was having a drink with one of the passengers – '

'What's that got to do with anything?' Luc asked.

Charles shrugged his shoulders. 'Miss Munro is a journalist, specializing in next-generation spacecraft. What she doesn't know about spaceships, you could write on your thumbnail. She thinks she felt a slight judder about two, two-and-a-half hours ago?'

Luc nodded.

'She said it was consistent with a solar panel blowing,' said Charles. 'And she thinks that just afterwards the ship changed course. If she's right, she's convinced the bad judder a little while ago was another solar panel blowing.'

'Has she told anyone else about this?' There was a wary tone in Luc's voice.

Charles shook his head.

'Where is she?' Luc wanted to know.

'Outside,' said Charles. 'I think you should – '

'Ask her to come in,' said Luc.

Charles strode to the door and a few seconds later ushered Fiona Munro into CNC.

Fiona Munro was as beautiful as she was brainy. Her perfectly cut hair framed the sort of face that turned men's heads.

'Lieutenant Mudrey tells me you need to talk to me,' said Luc. 'Would you like to fill me in?'

'Of course.' Fiona's voice was crisp. 'One of the solar panels shattered around noon, didn't it?'

'Noon plus five,' said Luc. 'Hit by a tiny asteroid.'

'An asteroid?'

'We were unlucky.' Luc's fist tightened. 'We had been warned that we were in danger of crossing an asteroid rush, but we took avoiding action.'

'That explains the dramatic increase in speed,' said Fiona. 'I am right. You did up your speed by a third or so two-and-a-half days ago?'

Cor van Boven nodded.

'Why did no one realize that the ship changed course after the panel blew?' Fiona sounded puzzled. 'Didn't anyone check in case the impact had thrown one of the nuclear engine's directional thrusters out of true?'

Luc nodded. 'The crew member responsible has been ordered to report to me,' he said.

'How long were we off course for, Captain?'

'Miss Munro, can I ask what all this is leading to?' Luc spoke through gritted teeth. '*NM* can operate on only a few panels. We've got six fully operative. As soon as we realized the directional thruster had been affected we took remedial action.'

Fiona held his gaze. 'If the angle of thrust of any of the fission engines was out by more than eight degrees, and if you took more than thirty minutes to make the correction, we're in serious trouble.'

'The angle was out ten degrees for more than half an hour,' muttered Davie.

'What sort of serious trouble?' Luc growled.

'If I can use a computer I'll show you.'

'You'll have to input manually,' said Giovanna Lorenzia. 'Your voice won't be registered in our user system.'

'Not a problem,' said Fiona. 'May I, Captain?'

'Be my guest!'

As Fiona sat in the chair facing the computer Luc pointed to, the others gathered around her.

Her hand flashed over the screen, touching box after box as she brought up diagram upon diagram, chart after chart, superimposing some on top of others, enlarging this one and reducing that. She then keyed in the command to bring up an image of the ship in one corner of the screen, showing it in perfect working order and on its true course to Mars.

'Now watch!' she said, changing the flightpath to account for the out-of-true engine.

'It changes path,' said Luc. 'We knew that.'

'Look at the solar panels!' Fiona said calmly. 'By themselves, the sudden change of direction and the huge increase in speed wouldn't have affected them. But the combination of the two ...'

'They're buckling,' gasped Charles.

'If I take the clock back to noon today let's see what happens,' said Fiona.

Everyone watched *New Millennium* on its true path as the clock moved from 12.00 hours but, as soon as it flicked over to show 12.05, one of the solar panels shattered.

'The asteroid. Now watch what happens next,' said Fiona. 'I'll speed it up.'

The clock zoomed around and, when it reached 14.30, a second panel exploded.

'That's Solar Panel Two,' said Davie. 'What happened to it?'

Fiona touched the freeze box and the graphics came to a standstill. 'The workload of the broken panel was transferred to the others. Normally, this isn't a problem. But it was transferred at the same time as the directional thruster went awry. The combined effect was to cause buckling in the remaining seven. The buckling and the strain of the extra workload shattered the second and its workload has now been transferred to the others.'

'They'll take it, surely?' said Cor van Boven.

'If they were in perfect working order, yes.' Fiona nodded. 'But they're buckled, remember . . .'

'We'd better cut off some of the working panels,' said Cor.

'Too late!' Fiona's voice showed no trace of emotion. 'As one panel breaks, the increased load on the others adds to the buckling, making it crack – slightly at first, then BANG!'

'How long have we got?'

Fiona restarted the clock and once again *NM* began to move along its projected flightpath vector.

When the clock reached 16.20 a third solar panel blew.

At 17.40 a fourth went and, after another hour had flashed by on the clock, the fifth followed suit.

A sixth went when the clock showed 19.30.

'I don't think I can take this,' gulped Davie.

'You're not the only one,' said Charles. 'Look, there goes the seventh at 20.10.'

The clock froze at 20.40 when the last solar panel blew and the *New Millennium* shuddered horribly before lurching wildly.

'What on earth can we do, Luc?' Cor van Boven's voice was shaking.

'There's only one thing you can do, Captain,' said Fiona.

'What's that?'

'Issue a Red Alert and abandon ship!'

CHAPTER 10

'How long have we got?' Cor van Boven gulped.

'No way of knowing,' said Fiona. 'We know we can't use the nuclear engines to get us to Mars. You won't have enough plutonium on board and even if you did, without the power from the solar panels, there would be an enormous strain on them. So strong a strain they could explode.'

'When?' asked Giovanna.

'No way of knowing,' said Fiona. 'This situation has never arisen before. Procedure is that if one or two solar panels go, no action need be taken. But if a third goes, speed must be cut – ' she looked at Luc.

'Twenty per cent,' he said quietly. 'And if a fourth goes, we must reduce by fifty per cent and head for the nearest base. Five we head for base at ten per cent speed and six we stop and issue a Mayday.'

'After that, you're in the realms of theory,' said Fiona. 'Even the best computer simulations never agree on what happens if seven or all eight go and the ship is running on nuclear power alone. The only thing they all do agree on is that if all eight go, the nuclear engines will eventually explode.'

'And there's no way of knowing when?' It was Charles who spoke.

'Taking the strain they'll be operating under after

the last panel blows will make them so volatile, they could go at any minute – or they could last for days.'

Every eye was on Luc.

'We have until 20.40 at the very latest,' he said. After a long pause and a glance at the clock on one of the computer screens, Luc went on, 'That's just over five hours from now. Lieutenant Mudrey, issue an immediate Mayday detailing our projected position every half hour from now onwards. If no one answers between now and 19.15 hours I want you to sound Abandon Ship. That should give us enough time to get the Emergency Escape Capsules well clear in case the ship blows up when the last panel goes.'

'But, Captain,' said Charles, 'some of the EECs are situated close to the solar panels. They may have been damaged by the explosions.'

Luc turned to Giovanna Lorenzia. 'Are there any ships within an hour or two of us?'

Giovanna's perfectly manicured nail tapped on one of the boxes at the top of the screen she was facing and almost at once, lines of data flashed on the screen. '*Amerigo Vespucci*'s the only one showing, sir,' she said. 'About an hour thirty away at top speed. She's trying to break her own record for the Mars-Moon run. If she does, she keeps the Blue Riband.'

'What frequency's she receiving on?'

Giovanna scanned the screen. 'She's not, sir,' she reported. 'She's on a receiving blackout.'

'You mean she won't get the Mayday?'

'She can't cut out Mayday frequencies,' said Giovanna. 'She'll get it.'

* * * * *

'Sir!' Senior Communications Officer Chester Sandberg III looked up from the screen, turned and beckoned to Admiral J. S. Bishop.

'Yes, Chester.' J.S. strode across the bridge of *Amerigo Vespucci*, the United States of the Two Americas' flagship Spacecruiser. 'What is it?'

'A Mayday, sir!'

'Mayday!' The unlit cigar J.S. constantly chewed on almost fell from his mouth. 'Where from?'

'Sector P59.XX/A.89/3.'

'Which, for the benefit of those of us who trained before this newfangled area designation system came in,' snapped J.S. 'is where?'

'25 million miles from Mars, sir.'

'Who's it from?'

'*New Millennium*, sir.'

'What! She can't possibly be in P59.XX/A.89/3 yet.' This time the cigar did fall from J.S.'s mouth, sending Bill Mitchell, the duty steward, scurrying across the bridge, dustpan in one hand, brush in the other, tut-tutting as he went. 'She's not due anywhere near there yet.'

'That's definitely where the signal's coming from,' Chester insisted. 'And it's definitely *New Millennium*.'

'If she's there already, then Dupont must be trying to break the record.' J.S. sounded thoughtful.

'Could you watch where you're going please, Admiral?' said a voice from the floor.

'What on earth are you doing down there, Doris?' asked J.S., using the nickname by which Bill Mitchell was known to everyone on board.

'Cleaning up after you, that's what I'm doing,' came the reply. 'That's all I ever do. Clean this. Wash that. Scrub the other. Would you look at my hands?'

'Shut up, Doris,' J.S. barked. 'Or I'll confiscate your curlers.'

'Hmph!' snorted Doris, brushing imaginary dust from an already spotless floor into an empty dustpan.

'According to the flightplan Luc Dupont logged before *NM* took off, he should still be in P56,' J.S. mused. 'If he's already at A.89/3 he's way ahead.' Admiral Jasper S. Bishop pretended to be all at sea with anything that was introduced within the past twenty years, but in reality he knew what he called 'the newfangled area designation system' as well as he knew the back of his hand.

He turned, almost tripping over the steward who was now rubbing at a tiny spot on the gleaming tiled floor. 'Doris,' he growled. 'Get out of the way!'

'My, my,' Doris sniffed. 'Who's being Mr Grumpy this afternoon?'

'Commander Buswell!' J.S. ignored the remark and nodded to the attractive brunette on his left. 'Increase speed by ten per cent.'

'And head for P59.XX/A.89/3?' she asked.

'Certainly not,' J.S.'s voice was thoughtful. 'I'm going to retain the Blue Riband if it's the last thing I do. Head for home at a constant speed of norm plus ten. If Luc Dupont thinks I'm going to fall for a cheap trick like issuing a Mayday to hold me up, he must think my middle name's Snow White.'

'You mean it's not?' came a voice from his feet.

CHAPTER 11

'Any response from *Vespucci*, Lieutenant?'

'None, sir!'

'What are they playing at?' snapped Luc.

'Can I say something, sir?'

'Yes, Davie.'

'When the panel went at 14.30, there was a fair shudder. When the next one goes, there'll be a bigger one. Right, Miss Munro?'

Fiona nodded.

'The passengers are going to start wondering what's up when there's a big bang a few minutes from now. I think we should tell them something has gone wrong but there's nothing to worry about.' Davie paused, then went on, 'But just in case, we're going to evacuate the ship. That way everyone will be safely aboard their EECs long before the last panels blow.'

'Good idea, Davie,' Luc said. 'Tell the crew to ask everyone to get to their EECs in an orderly fashion as quickly as possible.' He turned to Giovanna Lorenzia. 'And keep that Mayday going.'

* * * * *

'Hurry up, Christine! This is an emergency of some sort. They don't order us to go into the Emergency

Escape Capsules unless the ship's in real danger.'

'The steward said there was nothing to worry about.'

Believe that and you'll believe that spaghetti grows on trees.'

'You mean it doesn't?' Trixie looked at herself in the mirror. 'I'm ready. We're in EEC 60, aren't we?'

* * * * *

'Which EEC are we in?' Manda Jackson asked, strapping Janie into her harness.

'It was 50, wasn't it?' said Barney.

'No, it was 60,' the toddler already zipped into his life support suit piped up. 'I remember, 'cos it was the same as Grandpa's last birthday.'

'Good kid, Tom.' Barney ruffled his son's hair. 'Come on, Space Family Jackson. Let's get going.'

* * * * *

'Any answer to the Mayday yet, Giovanna?'

The Senior Navigation Officer shook her head.

'How about Mars? Any word?' Luc spoke in the same calm tone he would have used if he was asking his barber if his hair needed cutting at the back.

'Well, they know the situation,' Giovanna said.

'And they've launched a rescue mission. But we know that's not going to be even a twentieth of the way here before *NM*'s nuclear engines go into overload.'

* * * * *

Eileen Constable was in her bathroom when the third solar panel exploded at exactly 16.20. The force of the explosion was so strong that she was knocked to the floor of the shower. Too stunned to move for several seconds, she lay there, hot water streaming over her, before she got to her feet and finished washing her hair.

That done, she stepped from the cubicle and clambered into her flightsuit before making her way to EEC 60 as cool as a cucumber.

* * * * *

'Josh! Are you all right in there?'

'Let's just say I've been in more dignified situations.' Josh's voice echoed from the toilet he had been sitting in when the third panel solar blew. 'Could someone give me a clean pair of pants, please?' he said, opening the door a little.

His father rummaged in a drawer, found what he was looking for and put them in Josh's hand.

'I can't wear these.' Josh opened the door a

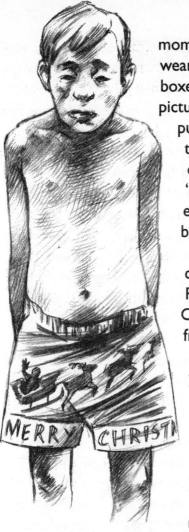

moment later and stood there wearing nothing but a pair of boxer shorts decorated with pictures of Santa Claus being pulled on his sleigh by a team of reindeer, bunches of holly and the words 'Merry Christmas' embroidered all round the bottom of the legs.

'They're the first pair I came across,' smiled Rowan. 'They were to be a Christmas surprise for you from your grandma.'

'You should see yourself,' giggled Sam.

'You should see the ones she bought you,' said Rowan.

'Let's just hope I live that long,' said Sam.

The lighthearted mood that Anne and Rowan had tried so hard to create in their cabin instantly evaporated and it was a very sombre Davis family who made their way to EEC 60.

CHAPTER 12

Most of New Millennium's Emergency Escape Capsules had berths for twenty passengers and five crew, with enough supplies to last fifty days. EEC 60, however, held eleven passengers and four crew although it was the same size as the others.

'The company always makes sure important senior employees have a little extra space no matter what the circumstances,' Professor Schultz had boasted to Trixie during the first emergency drill.

Now, he counted everyone aboard EEC 60. 'I think we're all here now,' he said.

The words were no sooner out of his mouth than a loud crash thundered through the EEC.

'Look out!' Sam shouted, throwing himself at his twin brother and knocking him to one side.

Just in time.

A moment later Josh would have been caught in a cascade of metal and broken glass raining into EEC 60 through a yawning gap in the ceiling.

* * * * *

'Let's get out of here!' shouted Rowan Davis. 'You and the baby first, Mrs Jackson, then Tom, the boys and the other women. Men last.'

Manda Jackson squeezed herself and Janie through the hatch and waited on the other side for Tom. But just then the EEC shuddered and a torrent of debris poured through the hole in the ceiling.

'It's all right, son,' said Barney, scooping the terrified toddler into his arms. 'No one's going to harm you. Come on – let's get you to Mummy.'

The boy clung to his father, sobbing loudly. 'Wanna stay with Daddy!' he screamed as Barney picked a path through the debris and pushed him into the mouth of the hatch where Trixie was standing.

'Gee, you're lucky, Tommy,' she said soothingly, kneeling down. 'You can walk through. The rest of us are gonna have to crawl.' And without a murmur of protest the little boy toddled through.

'Kids like me,' she said, shrugging her shoulders as Josh and Sam crawled through the hatch. 'OK, girls, let's do this alphabetically,' she said. 'You first, Annie, then you, Eileen. Come on. Quick now.' As soon as the other two women were through, Trixie got down on all fours and was about to get into the hatch when she turned and said, 'Schultzy, don't forget to bring my gold bag. It's got my make-up in it.'

'OK, guys, let's get out of here,' said Rowan when she was through.

'What now?' Professor Schultz looked around when Barney, Rowan and he were on the other side.

'Get to another EEC,' said Rowan. 'There's two more on the next level down.'

'Why was ours separate from the rest?' Trixie asked, fumbling in her bag for a lipstick.

'They're fixed to the side in upward-pointing V-shaped clusters,' said Sam. 'Eleven in each cluster. Lined up in pairs apart from the one at the point of the V, with the space between each pair widening the lower you go. So that when the engines are fired, the ones below won't be affected by the blast,' said Josh.

No sooner had he spoken than the door at the end of the corridor burst open and twenty or so men, women and children stampeded through it, the last one falling backwards, slamming the door shut.

'What's going on?' demanded Rowan Davis.

'Your EEC,' yelled the man leading the rush. 'Where is it?'

'Over there,' said Rowan. 'But it's badly damaged.'

'Not yours too?' said the man.

'Captain!' The tension in Davie Gillespie's voice was clear. 'Outside EEC 60. Screen nine.'

Luc stared at the screen, then flicked a switch on the side and leaned towards the voice box on the top. 'Mr Davis,' he said calmly. 'This is the Captain. Would you and the others with you please get to your EECs as quickly as possible.'

Rowan's lips moved.

'If you have anything to say, Mr Davis, talk towards the red light above the entry hatch to your EEC.'

A moment later Rowan's voice came down the line. 'Our EEC has been damaged.'

'And ours,' said the red-haired man beside him.

'Please stay where you are,' said Luc. 'Someone will be with you right away.'

'You know what you can do!' the man at Rowan's side spluttered. 'Come on, guys. Let's find another EEC.' And before Luc could say another word, the group who had burst into the passage raced for the door at the other end of the corridor.

'Look, Captain,' Davie shouted. 'Look at the screens for the top levels of EEC Formation 8.'

Luc watched in horror as each screen showed more and more people crawling out of the EECs into the corridors being scanned by the cameras.

'What's going on?' He shook his head as he spoke.

'I think I can answer that,' said Fiona Munro. 'The last solar panel that blew was directly above Formation 8, wasn't it?'

Luc nodded.

'I suspect the force of the explosion has damaged all the EECs on Formation 8's top three levels.'

'You mean – '

'I mean,' said Fiona, calmly, 'that each time a panel blows the same thing will happen to the EECs beneath it.'

'So, as the explosions get stronger and stronger, more and more levels will be damaged?'

It was Fiona's turn to nod. 'You can probably squeeze everyone whose EECs have been damaged into the ones below.'

'They'll be dangerously overloaded if we do,' groaned Luc.

'That's a risk we'll have to take,' said Fiona. 'And as soon as everyone's aboard you'll have to give the order to abandon ship.'

'If I don't?'

'There will be no way of getting even half of the people aboard to safety before the next panel blows.'

Fiona Munro was half-right. It wasn't just Formation 8 that had been damaged. The shock waves from the explosion had spread across as well as down the ship, damaging the first three levels of all the EEC formations.

And it wasn't long before Luc and the others knew it, for as the security cameras relayed their pictures back to CNC, the screens filled with pictures of panicking men, women and children rushing to find an undamaged EEC.

'What are we going to do, Captain?' asked Charles Mudrey.

'Get them down to Level Four or lower – '

'Not Level Four,' said Fiona Munro, looking at her watch. 'The next solar panel's going to explode in 30 minutes. When it does blow, it'll knock out the ones on Level Four.'

'Not if we launch them before the panel goes – the moment they're full!' cried Giovanna, her fingers flying furiously over the calculator on the screen by her left hand. 'If we fit an extra twelve or so into all the remaining capsules including Level Four's we should be all right.'

Wiping rivers of sweat from his brow, Luc sprang to the main communication computer. He brought up the details he needed and flashed orders to each senior crew member.

Then he reached for the master public address microphone. 'This is the Captain speaking,' he said. 'Would everyone please stand still and listen.'

He might as well have been blowing bubbles in the air for all the effect his words had.

The pictures on all the monitors bar one showed similar pictures as panic spread through the ship like wildfire. Terror-stricken passengers ran from level to level, determined to force their way into the first EEC they came to. The people already inside each capsule were equally determined to keep them out.

Fights were breaking out all over the ship as passengers punched, kicked and scratched each other in their desperation to find a safe place.

Only Rowan Davis and the others who had been in EEC 60 stood quite still.

'Only one thing for it,' said Luc.

'Hang on a mo,' Charles said. 'There's no reason why we or the Davis group should suffer.'

'You're right,' said Luc, flicking up two among a forest of switches by the red button in front of him. 'And remind me to apologize to the crew,' he went on as he pressed it.

The effect was instant.

All over the ship an intense, piercing, high-pitched whine stopped everyone in their tracks and froze

them to the spot,
their hands
clamped to
their ears in
a vain
attempt to shut
out the agonizing
sound.
Luc
took his
finger off
the button.
'This is
your Captain
speaking,' he said
into the public address system a moment or two
later. 'I regret to have to order you to abandon ship.'

Hands fell from ears to cover mouths that hung
open in astonished terror.

'There is no reason to panic,' Luc went on. 'A
senior member of the crew has been assigned to the
entrance of each Emergency Escape Capsule. Do
exactly as he or she says and a space will be found
for everyone. We may be a bit cramped inside but
help is already on the way from Mars.'

He paused for a moment to clear his throat.

'Now please do not panic and proceed to the
nearest EEC on levels four, five and six. Repeat. Please

proceed to the nearest EECs on levels four, five and six.'

Another pause. Another throat-clearing cough.

'I must inform you that my crew are armed and under orders to do whatever necessary, I repeat whatever necessary, to ensure a smooth and calm evacuation.'

* * * * *

'Better get down to Level Four,' said Rowan Davis. 'Come on!'

Everyone outside what was left of EEC 60 ran to the door the other passengers had burst through only a few minutes before.

Josh got to it first and pulled on the handle. 'It's stuck,' he cried.

'There's another door over there,' said Rowan, dashing towards it. 'Oh no!' he gasped a moment or two later. 'They've locked it.'

'Shultzy.' Trixie's voice was little more than a soft squeak. 'What does this mean?'

'It means', said Eileen Constable quietly, 'that we're trapped.'

* * * * *

'Schultzy! Do something!' Trixie's scream came down the line and echoed round Central Navigation Control.

'What the hell was that?' cried Luc.

'It's the lot from EEC 60,' said Charles. 'You didn't switch off the mike outside the capsule when you talked to them a minute or two ago, sir.'

Luc ran to the screen and leaned over the voice box. 'What's going on?' he rasped.

'The doors at either end of this corridor are locked, or jammed,' Rowan Davis answered.

Luc swivelled the lever by the side of the screen to change the camera angle.

'You're certain you can't open the doors?'

'Captain, do you think we'd still be here if we could?' snapped Schultz.

'Sorry, Professor,' said Luc. 'We'll send someone to get you out of there right away. We'll have you out and in an EEC as soon as we can.'

He switched off the mike and turned to Charles. 'Get someone up there right away.'

Charles raced to a free screen, and pressed the 'Crew Location' box. 'Get me the two crew closest to EEC 60,' he said to the computer.

'Please!'

'Please get me the two crew closest to EEC 60.'

'Junior Communications Officer Nathan Gulliver PI Number 8524, and Flight-Sergeant Astrid Tandy.'

'How's it going, sir?' Charles turned back to Luc, who was seated by a bank of screens showing what was happening in various parts of the ship.

'Looks as though order has been restored.'

Charles looked at picture after picture of New Millennium's crew members shepherding horrified passengers along the corridors towards EECs. Each one guided as many as possible into a capsule before moving on to the next.

'How long before the next panel goes?'

'Ten minutes forty,' said Giovanna, glancing at the clock on the corner of the screen.

'Who's the Senior Officer on Level Four?'

Giovanna repeated the question to the computer, remembering to add 'Please'.

'Sub-Lieutenant Steiffel, PI Number 2536.'

Luc punched Steiffel's number into his handset.

'Sub-Lieutenant Ethan Steiffel here, sir!'

'Brief me on the situation on Level Four, please.'

'Thirteen of the fourteen EECs are now completely full, apart from assigned crew members.'

'You have allowed for extra crew as well, in each one?'

'Of course, sir.'

'Fill the last EEC, get all crew to their stations, and as soon as they're all in give the order to launch.

You have – ' Luc glanced at his wristwatch – 'nine minutes thirty seconds.'

'That's not a problem,' said Ethan.

'And make sure the senior crew member in each EEC knows his or her orders – speed, rendezvous co-ordinates, formation pattern.'

'They have all been thoroughly briefed, sir.'

'Good man, Ethan,' said Luc. 'I know I can depend on you to do things by the book.'

* * * * *

'What's that noise?' Josh moved away from the door he had been desperately trying to open.

'Sound's like someone's trying to break it down,' said Rowan.

The same prayer was on everyone's lips. 'Please, God, let them get us out of here.'

The same expression of hope appeared in everyone's eyes.

Everyone, that is, apart from two.

Tom Jackson, who was too young to realize the desperate situation he and the others were in.

And baby Janie, who was sound asleep in her mother's arms.

CHAPTER 14

'Bad news, I'm afraid, sir,' Nathan's voice came through Luc's headset. 'The doors are totally jammed and there's no way we can break through them.'

'OK, Nathan. Thanks for trying. Best get yourselves down to Level Five or Six quickest,' Luc went on. 'The E –'

Before Luc could tell Nathan that the EECs on Level Four had just been launched, there was a loud rumbling and a moment later the ship was rocked by an explosion that sent a sent a tremor of destruction rippling round *NM*.

In the corridor outside EEC 60 Trixie Russell was thrown hard against Josh, knocking the wind out of him as he tumbled to the floor.

A huge crack appeared in the wall Manda Jackson was leaning against, and if it hadn't been for her husband's lightning-quick reactions she would have fallen into the black void beyond.

In Central Navigation Control, steel uprights buckled so badly that the shelves they were supporting twisted, sending millions of Euros' worth of equipment crashing to the floor in a blizzard of breaking glass.

'I don't think we should be around when the next panel goes,' said Davie Gillespie, putting into words what everyone else in CNC was thinking.

'How long have we got before the next one goes?' Luc looked at Fiona Munro.

'An hour,' she answered.

'Ethan!' Luc shouted into a voice mike. 'How badly affected are you down there?'

'Not much physical damage, sir,' came the reply. 'But the passengers can't take much more. And I don't think the crew can either.'

'Get everyone into an EEC as quickly as possible. As many as they'll take. Even if they're crammed in like sardines, the passengers probably have more chance than if we delay.'

'Yes, sir.'

'And once everyone else is safely away, get to my EEC as quickly as you can. Start her up so that the moment everyone in CNC gets there, we can take off.'

'We're forgetting two things, sir,' said Charles Mudrey. 'Professor Schultz and the others – '

'And?'

'The serum!'

Luc clasped his hands together and held them to his lips as if he were praying. 'Let's deal with the easy one first,' he said eventually. 'Lieutenant Mudrey. Get down to the Freezer Unit. Put the serum in a thermal bag and take it straight to my EEC. It's on Level Ten. Well below the others.'

'Right away, sir.' Charles shot out of the CNC.

'Mr van Boven,' Luc turned to Cor. 'We're going to have to cut one of these doors open. How thick's the steel?'

'Five point zero eight centimetres, sir.'

'Get to the armoury and find me a grade-three laser gun,' Luc drummed his fingers on the arm of his chair as he spoke. 'That should do it.'

'We don't have a grade-three laser on board, sir.'

Luc groaned loudly. 'Then there's nothing we can do for them,' he said, his voice breaking.

'I think there may be,' cried Giovanna, looking up from one of the few remaining working screens facing her. 'Look, sir.'

Luc's eyes took in the picture of Rowan Davis and the others, slumped on the floor, a look of hopelessness on all their faces.

'What am I meant to be looking at?'

'The gap in the wall beside the woman with the baby. It's a ventilation shaft,' said Giovanna, touching one of the command boxes. Almost immediately an outline of New Millennium criss-crossed by a network of red and green lines flashed onto the screen.

The Senior Navigation Officer reached for one of the boxes running down the side.

Two tiny specks of yellow appeared, one on Level One and another on Level Ten.

'The dot on Level One is the gap by Mrs Jackson,' said Giovanna. 'The one on Level Ten is the ventilation grille just along from the entry hatch to your EEC. If they can get into the ventilation system, they could climb down to Level Ten and we could get them out there!'

Luc streaked back to his control centre and flicked a switch.

'Mr Davis,' he shouted into the voice mike. 'Can you hear me?'

There was no response.

'Oh, no!' Luc croaked. 'The last explosion must have knocked out the communications link with Level One. There's no way of getting them out now!'

It was Cor van Boven who noticed strands of loose wire dangling below the Captain's control panel.

'Try again, sir,' he said after he had replaced them. And this time, when Luc asked Rowan Davis if he could hear him, everyone trapped on Level One looked up and stared into the camera.

'Yes, Captain,' said Rowan, 'I can hear you loud and clear.'

'Thank goodness for that. I think there's a way we can get you out of there.'

'How?' several voices gasped in unison.

'The gap in the wall along from Mrs Jackson. If you can all squeeze through it you'll be in the ventilation system,' Luc explained. 'You've got to climb down to the fifth horizontal duct you'll come to. It's wide and high enough for you to walk along. Get to the next vertical shaft and then climb down it past another three ducts. Enter the next one you come to and, by the time you get there, someone will have opened the ventilation grille next to my EEC and can escort you to it. Got that?'

Rowan nodded and repeated the instructions.

'You've got fifty minutes,' said Luc. 'Good luck.'

* * * * *

Each of the rungs riveted into the ventilation shaft was made of luminous steel and glowed in the dark. By the time Rowan, who was in the lead, was fifteen metres down and had passed the mouths of the first two shafts he had developed a rhythm – right hand down to the next rung, left foot down to the next rung, left hand to right hand, right foot to left foot, right hand down, left foot down ...

'Last man in,' called Barney, who had used the belt of his life-support suit to tie Tom to his back. 'All right, Manda?' he went on.

'No problems,' replied his wife, who was just behind Rowan.

Rowan passed the third duct and a few minutes later the fourth, then the fifth.

'I've just passed the duct we've got to walk along-long-long.' His voice echoed up the shaft. 'It's on the right, like the others. I'll go below it and come in last.'

He watched as Manda, followed by Josh and Sam,

clambered into the duct.

'How're you doing, darling?' Anne Davis looked down at her husband as she crossed to the duct.

'I'll be glad when we're aboard the Captain's EEC,' he said.

'We'll get out of here. Don't worry,' said Rowan. And they did.

It seemed to take forever but they made it to the open ventilation grille on Level Ten where Luc was waiting for them. 'We've got ten minutes,' he said as he helped them out. 'Plenty of time.'

That said, he turned to Davie who, along with everyone else, had left CNC a few minutes earlier to make his way to the Captain's Emergency Escape Capsule. 'Any sign of Charles?'

Cor shook his head.

'Where is he?' Luc drummed his fingers on the wall beside the open ventilation grille. 'Where's he got to? He should be here by now.'

At that moment Lieutenant Charles Mudrey was sprawled unconscious on the floor of the Freezer Centre, the phial of serum a few centimetres from his outstretched fingers.

CHAPTER 16

Fiona was the first of the Captain's party to squeeze through the hatch into the Captain's EEC. 'Charles, how did you get in here without anyone seeing?' cried Fiona to the flight-suited figure standing at the far end of the EEC, his back to her.

But it wasn't Charles.

'Who are you?' she cried as the figure slowly turned round.

'Ethan Steiffel at your service, ma'am.'

'Hi, Ethan,' breathed Giovanna, squeezing past Fiona.

'Giovanna! How you doin'?'

'Be glad when I wake up from this particular nightmare,' she replied. 'Charles Mudrey hasn't come aboard yet, has he?' she went on.

Ethan shook his head.

'He'd better get here quickly,' said Fiona. 'The next panel's about to go.'

* * * * *

When Luc had ordered Charles to get the serum, he had no idea of what conditions were like on Level Eight where the Freezer Centre was located. The explosion that had devastated much of *NM* had ripped through the corridors on that level. Most of the panels were blown off the walls.

So much debris littered the floor that Charles almost lost his balance and toppled over several times before he eventually reached the Freezer Unit.

He wrenched open the door and darted across to the compartment in which the phial was stored. Pulling it out, Charles was about to drop it into the thermal bag he took from a drawer when, with no warning whatsoever, a panel fell from the ceiling above. It caught him on the back of the neck and sent him tumbling to the floor.

When he came to a few seconds later, the only thing he recalled was the captain telling him to get to the EEC on Level Ten. Weaving like a drunken sailor, he managed to get out of the Freezer Unit, with no recollection that he had left the vital serum behind.

* * * * *

When Junior Ensign Paddy O'Dwire heard the order to abandon ship, he ran towards the EEC he had been assigned to on Level Five. He was almost there when he remembered he had left the only thing he really treasured – his grandfather's gold watch – in his quarters on Level Eight.

No way am I going without it, he said to himself.

Pulling open one of the doors that led to a flight

of emergency stairs he raced down, taking them two and three at a time until he reached Level Eight. He dashed to his sleeping quarters, grabbed the watch from the top of the cabinet by his bed and thrust it into the pocket of his flight-suit.

He raced back into the corridor and straight into Charles Mudrey, sending him crashing to the floor.

'Sorry, sir,' coughed Paddy, helping Charles to his feet. 'Are you all right?'

'Gotta get to Level Ten. Captain's EEC,' Charles said groggily, before slumping to the floor.

Only one thing for it, Paddy said to himself, and somehow managed to drape the unconscious officer over his shoulders.

Stumbling several times and staggering under Charles's weight, Paddy struggled down two flights of stairs, and had just made it along the passage that led to Luc Dupont's EEC when his legs buckled.

'What's happening?' cried Luc, running to help.

'It's Lieutenant Mudrey, sir. I found him – '

'Never mind where you found him,' barked Luc. 'Just get him into the capsule.'

They sat Charles in the entry hatch and pushed him in before crawling through the opening.

'Charles,' said Luc, gently tapping him on the face to bring him around. 'Where's the phial?'

'Phial?' moaned Charles, his eyes fluttering open. 'What phial?'

Luc's lips moved, but no one heard what he said. At that precise moment, yet another solar panel exploded with such force that the whole ship shuddered violently. Everyone in the capsule tumbled around like coffee beans in a grinder.

As Trixie reached out for something to steady herself, her hand grabbed a handle sticking out of the wall beside the entry hatch.

'No!' cried Luc, throwing himself at her. 'Let go!'

But it was too late.

The EEC's inner hatch slammed shut and, with a loud grating noise, the supports holding the EEC to the side of the ship fell away.

With an ominous rumble, the EEC's engines blazed into life and, with a loud roar, it raced up the outer shell of the mother ship and shot into space.

CHAPTER 17

'Admiral. Better come quick!'

'What is it?' J.S. ran across the bridge.

'It's *New Millennium*, sir. She's launched her EECs.'

The Admiral's face turned white as he looked at the screen and saw dot after dot shooting away from the larger circle in the middle of the screen.

'Great balls o' fire!' he shouted. 'The Mayday was genuine. Change course and head for – ' He looked at the location indicator – 'P59.XX/A.89/3.5. With all possible speed!'

* * * * *

'We've got to go back for the serum,' shouted Luc, floating beside Cor who had been thrown towards the control panel by the force of the unexpected take-off. 'Stop this thing and do an about-turn. The rest of you strap yourselves in as soon as you can.'

Cor keyed in the necessary command and a moment later the EEC was streaking back towards *New Millennium*.

'We didn't go through proper take-off procedures,' said Cor. 'We won't be able to dock.'

'No problem,' said Luc. 'Take her in as close as you can. Ethan, Paddy and Davie, get your Manned

Manoeuvring Units on – you're coming with me.'

'But they don't know where the serum is.' Giovanna clenched her fists as she spoke. 'Only Lieutenant Mud – '

'I remember now, sir,' Charles interrupted her. 'I'd just taken it out of the freezer when something fell on me,' he went on, rubbing his head. 'It rolled underneath. I'd better come with you.'

'You're in no fit state to do anything.' Luc shook his head. 'Stay here.'

Charles tried to protest as Luc and the others clambered into the suits that would allow them to travel untethered through space, but Luc was adamant.

'I'm as close as I dare go, sir,' shouted Cor.

'How far out?'

'One hundred metres.'

'Maintain this position until we get back,' said Luc. Then he put on his helmet and beckoned the other three to follow him to the emergency hatch.

As soon as Ethan – who was bringing up the rear – was inside the hatch, Giovanna slammed the door shut and the four men squeezed down the short corridor to the hatch at the other end of the airlock. Luc flicked the red switch set into the wall and the hatch slid open. They stepped out into space. *New Millennium* was so enormous that even from one hundred metres away all Luc could see in front of him

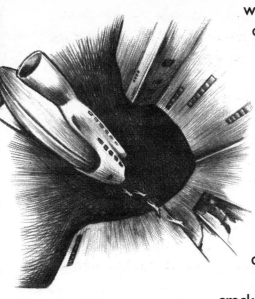

was a vast expanse of metal that seemed to stretch forever.

He fired the rocket pack and zoomed towards his doomed ship.

'All right?' he asked into the voice box set into the visor covering his face.

Three 'Yes, sirs' crackled into his earset, and the four men shot towards *NM*.

'Looks as though all the hatches are shut,' said Ethan as they closed in.

'No,' said Luc. 'There's a gap in the fuselage over there, below that shattered solar panel. Head for it.'

What looked from a distance like a narrow crack running down the side of the doomed ship widened as the four closed in. By the time they reached it they could see there was just enough room for them to get through into Level Two beyond.

'Level Eight,' said Luc, heading for the nearest lift.

'That's not going anywhere.' Paddy stared at the tattered metal door, twisted half-open to reveal the shattered remains of the car beyond.

'Stairs!' cried Luc, lumbering towards the door. 'Hope they haven't been damaged.' Luc tugged the heavy steel door open. 'Nope! They're fine. Come on.'

The four men made their way down the stairs as fast as their cumbersome suits would let them.

'Here we are,' yelled Ethan, who was faster than the others. 'Level Ei – '

The word froze on his lips when he took in the sight that met his eyes.

More panels had fallen from the wall, several of the tubes fixed to the wall behind had ruptured and showers of sparks rained down from the ceiling.

'Over there,' shouted Luc, who was just behind.

Keeping to one side to stay clear of the glittering cascade, the four men stumbled along the corridor to the door at the far end which flapped backwards and forwards as they pushed their way through it.

'The serum could be anywhere.' Davie looked around, taking in the mess that met his eyes.

'There.' Luc pointed to the floor. 'A thermal bag.'

As he went to pick it up, the clock on the wall flicked over from 19.29 to 19.30 and, exactly as Fiona Rivers had predicted, the sixth panel blew with a force that sent all four men flying around the room.

CHAPTER 18

As the ship rocked violently to and fro, the four men struggled to get to their feet.

'Look!' shouted Paddy, pointing to something rolling out from under the freezer compartment. 'It's the phial.'

'Zip it in your pocket, Paddy,' Luc said. 'And let's get the hell out of here.'

Going as fast as they could, they retraced their steps out of the Freezer Centre, along the corridor and back to the staircase. But when they opened the door leading to it, looks of horror spread across the faces of all four.

'Now what?' said Paddy, gazing at the twisted pieces of metal which were all that remained of the steps that had run between Level Eight and Level Seven above.

'There's another staircase, the other side of the Freezer Centre.' Ethan's voice came through the others' headsets. 'Let's get going.'

'Thank goodness for that,' gasped Davie when they reached the second flight of stairs and saw it was unharmed by the last explosion.

'Give us a hand, someone,' cried Paddy as the other three began to trundle up the steps. 'My rocket pack's caught on this piece of metal.' Ethan and Davie were about to go back when they heard Paddy say, 'No, it's all right – I've done it.'

It seemed to take forever to climb back up to Level Two but they made it. 'This way,' panted Luc. 'The gap's over there.'

One by one the four men squeezed through the hole on *NM*'s fuselage. 'Blast,' said Paddy, who was last. 'I've done it again.'

'What?' A voice filled his helmet.

'Caught my backpack.'

'Want a hand?'

'No, it's all right, one more tug'll do it.'

'Hurry up,' said Luc. 'We don't want to be hanging around out here when the next panel blows.'

By the time Paddy had freed himself, Luc and the others had reached the EEC and were opening the outer door of the entry hatch.

'Wait for me,' joked Paddy as he fired his rocket pack and set off to join them.

But before he had gone twenty metres there was a loud crackling sound from his backpack and he shot upwards at alarming speed.

'AAAAAGHH!' His terrified scream echoed round the helmets of his three colleagues.

'What the –' shouted Luc.

'Paddy!' yelled Davie, seeing the young Irishman flash past him.

'My rocket pack!' screamed Paddy. 'I must have

damaged it when I caught it on one of those bits of metal. It's out of control.'

'Hang on, we're coming,' cried Davie.

But it was useless.

Power surged uncontrollably through the pack, sending the junior ensign first one way then another, shooting upwards, plunging downwards, twisting and spinning like a wasp trapped in a jar.

'What's he doing now?' shouted Luc as Paddy flashed past him, desperately trying to unzip the pocket on the front of his suit.

'It's the serum!' yelled Ethan a few moments later, seeing what Paddy was now holding in his hand.

As the terrified Irishman roared past Ethan, he let the phial go and it drifted through space. Ethan managed to reach out and wind his fingers around it.

'Paddy!' Ethan and Davie heard Luc shout.

'Can't take – ' Whatever it was he was going to say next was drowned out by a loud rumble as more and more power roared through his rocket pack, sending him soaring upwards.

Powerless to help, Luc, Ethan and Davie watched as he grew smaller and smaller and smaller and then vanished completely from sight.

* * * * *

'Where's Paddy?' Cor asked as soon as Luc and the others had crawled back into the EEC.

'He didn't make it,' said Luc and explained what had happened. 'But if it wasn't for him, the serum would still be in his pocket, and we'd never get it to Mars, even if it will be too late to save everyone now.'

'Poor boy,' breathed Trixie. 'How long will he stay conscious?'

Luc shook his head. 'He should have enough oxygen to last for two, three hours. When it starts to run low he'll get groggy, until it dries up completely and he'll ... ' he felt a lump in his throat and had to swallow hard to suppress it. 'He'll black out and ... '

Everyone sat in silence, the same picture in their mind's eye – a ghostly suited figure floating in space for ever and ever.

Fiona Munro spoke first. 'I think we should get away from here fast. The next panel's going to go any minute.'

'Quite right.' Luc collected his thoughts and

strapped himself into his seat. 'Give it everything she's got, Cor. The others won't wait for us forever.'

* * * * *

'Rendez-vous point coming up, Captain,' said Davie Gillespie who was at the controls.

'Contact the senior officer aboard each EEC,' Luc said. 'Tell them to get into flight formation and proceed to sector T72.AB/87/2 to meet up with the rescue fleet from Mars.'

'How long till we get there?' asked Trixie.

'At least five weeks.'

'Five weeks,' groaned Trixie. 'What *am* I going to wear?'

'There's plenty of clean clothes aboard,' said Luc.

'Thank goodness for that,' sighed Josh.

Fiona Munro looked at her watch. 'Twenty to nine. If I was right, the last panel's just blown.'

'You've been spot on so far,' said Charles.

'It's not just the last solar panel that's exploded,' shouted Ethan, who was standing by a porthole at the back of the EEC. 'Look!'

Even from more than a thousand kilometres away, the series of enormous flashes and sheets of flame shooting out in all directions were clearly visible as New Millennium's nuclear engines blew.

'Wow!' gasped Josh, as a vast finger of flame

burst from the huge ball of fire.

No sooner had he spoken than the capsule
began to shake like a pneumatic drill.

'I can't handle it,' yelled Davie. 'She's being blasted
way off course.'

'Not just us,' cried Cor, looking at a screen. 'The
whole fleet's in chaos.'

As he spoke another capsule shot past, missing
Luc's EEC by less than fifty metres. A few seconds
later, it slammed nose-first into one spinning madly

out of control just behind.

'There's dozens of people in those capsules,' shouted Charles. 'We've got to do something.'

'There's nothing we can do,' yelled Luc. 'They wouldn't know what hit them.'

'There goes another one,' screamed Trixie, her hand flying to her mouth as the burning debris smashed into a third EEC, which shuddered like a jelly before exploding into a million pieces.

'I can't watch.' Anne Davis buried her head in her husband's shoulder, as two more capsules collided and burst into flames. 'Those poor people,' she sobbed.

'How's it going, Davie?' Luc yelled to his second in command, who was desperately trying to bring the EEC under control.

Davie wasn't the only senior officer wrestling with the controls of an EEC.

Throughout the fleet, officer after officer was frantically trying to prevent his or her capsule being thrown first one way then another by the huge blast. But it was useless. Not only had the tattered fleet been scattered like autumn leaves on a windy day, the communications systems on some capsules were damaged beyond repair. On others the navigation equipment had been smashed to smithereens.

Unable to regroup, the capsules shot through space. Their passengers were left with hardly a shred of hope between them.

CHAPTER 19

'We're going to die, aren't we?' wailed Trixie for the hundredth time.

'Shut up, Christine,' snapped Professor Schultz. 'You're getting on everyone's nerves.'

Luc glanced round the cabin.

For five days now he and his crew had done what they could to keep everyone's spirits up, but as time passed tempers had started to fray. Even the usually calm Anne Davis had burst into tears when little Tom Jackson asked his father when they were going home.

'Any luck raising any of the others, Davie?' he called.

Davie was about to reply when a voice boomed down the line. 'Come in, *New Millennium* EEC I,' it echoed around the capsule.

'What the – ' Luc headed for the communication panel. 'This is Captain Luc Dupont,' he said into the voice box. 'Who am I talking to? Over.'

'Chester Sandberg III,' came the reply. 'On board *Amerigo Vespucci*. We have you on screen and will be with you in thirty minutes. Prepare to dock your vehicle with us. Over.'

'Understood,' said Luc calmly, then punched the air. Sam and Josh whooped with joy, Barney soothed his sobbing wife, Anne and Rowan Davis hugged each other, Trixie squeezed the Professor so hard he started to go blue and Eileen Constable looked up from the book she had been reading, her lips showing the slightest suspicion of a smile.

* * * * *

'Welcome to *Amerigo Vespucci*, Captain,' J.S. saluted Luc as he clambered out of the hatch after everyone else on board had left the capsule. 'I'm afraid I must ask you to report to the sick bay right away to be tested for radiation exposure. I'll escort you.'

'Shouldn't need to,' said Luc. 'All our EECs are equipped with deflector shields.'

'That was a heck of a bang,' J.S. said. 'Better safe than sorry.'

'How many others have you rescued?' Luc asked as the two men made their way to a lift.

'How many were launched?'

'Forty-two, I think. Forty-three, maybe.'

'We've found twenty-five capsules, and have located another twelve.'

'We lost five when *NM* exploded,' Luc said. 'Thank goodness it wasn't more.'

As the lift door slid open, Luc glanced at the man already in it. 'How the – ' he gasped, unable to believe his eyes.

'Captain Dupont,' the man said.

'Paddy?' spluttered Luc. 'It can't be.'

'My rocket pack sorted itself out and I was picked up by one of the other EECs,' explained Paddy. 'Million to one chance.'

'And the rest?' said Luc.

'Captain,' Paddy looked down at his feet. 'Will there be an inquiry?'

'Bound to be, son,' said J.S. 'That was one of the most expensive explosions in history.'

'And there's no way of getting the serum to Mars on time,' said Luc.

'Serum?' J.S. sounded puzzled. 'What serum?'

'The antidote to the virus that's knocking them out on Mars.'

'When's it got to be there?'

When Luc told him, J.S. clapped him on the back and said, 'Can't guarantee to get it there by then, but it won't be long after.'

'That's impossible!' cried Luc.

'No it's not.' There was a smirk on J.S.'s face. 'Ever heard of solar sails?'

'Yes, but they're still on the drawing board.'

'Officially, yes,' said J.S. 'But we've got a prototype on board. We were testing it around Mars.'

'And?'

'And they work. That babe's the fastest thing in space.'

*****

'Goodbye, Captain.'

More than five weeks had passed since Luc and the others had been taken aboard *Amerigo Vespucci*.

The serum had got to Mars late, but in time to get a mass inoculation programme underway before it was too late.

Packed to the gunwales, the *Amerigo Vespucci* carried everyone to Mars and now they were there, it was time for goodbyes.

'Goodbye, Professor Schultz,' said Luc, shaking the professor's hand.

'I can't think what's keeping Miss Russell.' The Professor looked at his watch. 'Oh, here she is now.'

Luc looked to his right and saw Trixie coming towards him.

'Captain, sweetie. Goodbye,' Trixie gushed and, before Luc could do anything about it, kissed him on the lips, leaving them smeared with her bright crimson lipstick.

'Red Alert, Captain?' said Doris Mitchell who happened to be passing. 'Not your colour at all!'

MARS

Of the nine planets in the solar system, Mars, the 'Red Planet', is the next out from Earth and the only one likely to be colonized by humans.

GETTING THERE

The Russians were the first to send spacecraft to Mars to find out what the Red Planet was like. After several unsuccessful attempts, in 1962 they succeeded in flying *Mars 1* to within 193,000 kilometres of the planet, but radio contact was lost soon after.

During the late 1970s and early 1980s, the US *Viking* missions added to our store of knowledge about the planet.

Most successful of all Mars missions to date was the 1997 United States *Pathfinder* mission. When it touched down, a mobile rover called *Sojourner* was released to explore the planet. Equipped with cameras and scientific instruments, the rover roamed the surface around the lander and sent back millions of nuggets of information. These are still being pored over at NASA headquarters where scientists are looking forward to the day when there will be human colonies on Mars.

Another step in achieving this is the *Mars Global Surveyor*, a spacecraft that began mapping the planet's surface in 1998. It will also examine mineral reserves with pinpoint accuracy. Future craft will measure how the percentages of the gases that make up the Martian atmosphere vary from season to season.

ROBOTS

NASA believe that robots will be landed on Mars. These will send back information over several years about the possibility of earthquake activity in various parts of the planet. They will also tell us about the presence of water and mineral resources in much more detail than is possible with current spacecraft.

SMART SURFACE ROVERS

These are essential for Martian exploration. Working independently and thinking for themselves, SSRs will roam the planet, gathering samples of surface materials, laying instruments on or beneath the ground and transmitting data back to an orbiting spacecraft from where it will be forwarded back to Earth.

Human Expeditions

Humans are likely to step on to Mars towards the end of the twenty-first century. One NASA forecast has them using a nuclear-electric spacecraft equipped with a lander that would carry a crew of five to Mars, land them on the surface and bring them back to Earth. The nuclear-electric propulsion system will be powered by two-megawatt nuclear reactors.

Built-in air supplies, water and life-support systems and artificial gravity would keep the crew going throughout the flight.

The actual spacecraft will probably be assembled on the International Space Station or one of its successors. When it is finished it will then be put into orbit around the Earth where its crew would board it for the long journey to Mars. Alternatively, it may be flown to a base on the Moon from where it would be launched.

The reason for launching rockets bound for Mars either from Earth orbit or from the Moon is that a spacecraft launched from orbit or beyond doesn't need to carry the fuel required to overcome the Earth's gravity and air resistance.

Scientists reckon that the first Martian astronauts will take around 550 days from launch until they are in orbit around the planet. There, they will stay for most of the 100-day mission, only landing for around thirty days to make the first human explorations of the Red Planet.

It will be many years, perhaps decades, after this before the next stage – the establishment of permanent Martian bases – will begin. By then increasingly efficient nuclear engines will have cut the journey time from fourteen months to around three.

At first, these bases will be small. They will house between ten and 100 people whose jobs will be to explore and survey the planet and conduct experiments and small engineering projects.

THE COST

NASA estimates that the cost of developing nuclear rockets and the other technology necessary to take us to Mars could be as much as $500 billion. This is far too much for any one country to afford on its own. So it is likely that missions to Mars will be joint ventures between several nations.

SOLAR CELLS

Solar cells have been used since the 1960s to power spacecraft by turning the power of sunlight directly into electricity. They have no moving parts to break down or wear out, they produce no noise, no fumes or any other waste products.

They will continue to be used throughout the next century on spacecraft bound for Mars and will be the main power source when we come to build colonies on Mars.

SOLAR SAILS

NASA is already drawing up plans for a spaceship so fast it could cut the journey time for a mission to Mars from nearly four years at present to just a few months.

Scientists working at the United States' Jet Propulsion Laboratory believe that aluminium sails that harness the solar wind may be the only way to cross the vast expanse of space should we ever wish to reach for the stars. Conventional rockets, even the most powerful nuclear ones, would be far too slow and would not have enough capacity to carry the enormous quantities of fuel needed for such a journey.

The starship's energy could come from a sun-powered laser focused on the sail through a huge 100-kilometre-diameter orbiting lens close to Mercury, the planet nearest to the Sun. Scientists believe this could accelerate the spacecraft to a tenth of the speed of light or 30,000 kilometres a second.